An Athlete's Fantasy

R AYMOND F ELL

authorHOUSE®

AuthorHouse™
1663 Liberty Drive, Suite 200
Bloomington, IN 47403
www.authorhouse.com
Phone: 1-800-839-8640

First published by AuthorHouse 8/5/2008

ISBN: 978-1-4343-9483-5 (sc)

Printed in the United States of America
Bloomington, Indiana

This book is printed on acid-free paper.

DEDICATION

This book is dedicated to people who, like the inventor in the story, live their lives with a strong feeling of confidence that they can accomplish what they set out to do. They set goals for themselves and then strive to do their best to attain them. Many obstacles may surface, but they just keep their eyes on the prize.

FOREWORD

An Athlete's Fantasy is a story that extends beyond the realm of possibilities, but the author has readers believing every word of it. What athlete would not want to possess that which the story's inventor produces? He has drastically changed the world of some major sports at every level.

Whether you enjoy jogging, road racing, basketball, football, boating or just plain walking to lose weight, the author has you in mind as you go through the book.

It is the author's wish that readers place themselves in the action that takes place throughout the story. This could make a big difference in the degree of enjoyment they would derive from it. The author believes that the vivid imagination portrayed in this book can be an excellent antidote for escaping the constant barrage of disconcerting news to which we are all daily subjected in our world today.

Chapter One

Jeremy was in his mid-fifties when, one summer day, he decided to go over to the school track near his home and run around it a few times. When he reached about the half way mark, he felt he couldn't run anymore, so he walked the rest of the quarter mile and went home. Upon his arrival there, his wife Geraldine asked, "How did you make out?"

"Not so well," remarked Jeremy, still breathing heavily. "I'll give it another try tomorrow."

"Don't you think you're kind of old for this sort of thing?"

"Not really, I feel I'm in good health and Dr. Whiting gave me a clean bill of health just last week. I told him I wanted to do some running and he encouraged me wholeheartedly."

The next day, Jeremy went over to the track again and ran around it without stopping. He was pleased with that and then decided to walk around one more time.

For the next couple of weeks, Jeremy visited the track every morning and would gradually increase the number of times he would circle it. Before he realized it, he had built up his endurance enough to run a mile without stopping. Jeremy preferred to do these workouts alone. He felt that way he could run at his own pace and stop whenever he felt he had done enough.

After about a month of these daily runs, Jeremy was now doing two miles a day and feeling pretty good about what he was accomplishing. As he was running along one morning, another runner pulled up alongside him and asked, "Would you be interested in entering a road race on Saturday?"

"I've never been in one. I don't know much about them."

"Your pace looks good, you should be able to do alright," the other man said encouragingly.

"What's your name?" asked Jeremy.

"Phil," the man replied, "and I would be happy to pick you up on Saturday morning."

"That sounds great, by the way, where is this race, what time does it begin and how long is it?"

"It's a 5K in Braintree at 9A.M. I'll need your name, address and telephone number."

"My name is Jeremy. I'll give you my card. It has my telephone number on it. I live right in that white house over there," answered Jeremy as he pointed to it,

"I'll be waiting for you."

The next morning over breakfast, Jeremy mentioned to Geraldine that he was going to be in a road race on Saturday and this fellow Phil, whom he met on the track, was going to do the driving.

"Are you sure you're ready for road racing? You have only been running a short while."

"I feel I'm ready, I'll just pace myself and make sure I don't overdo."

"Do you know how much it will cost and what you'll wear?"

"Yes, Phil called me last night and filled me in on a lot of the details, I had a chance to question him quite a bit about road racing in general, since he's been in so many."

When Saturday morning arrived, Phil was at Jeremy's house bright and early.

"Are you nervous about this being your first race?" Phil asked, as Jeremy got in the car.

"No, I feel great," as he rubbed his sleepy eyes, "I'm really glad you asked me to join you. I don't know when I might have entered a race, if you hadn't told me about this one."

"How long have you been running road races, Phil," asked Jeremy as they were driving along.

"About ten years now, but I still remember my first one. It was on a rainy day, everyone got soaked. We were running through some pretty deep puddles, I recall. The finish line was a happy sight that day, believe me!"

After they reached the school where the race was being held, they proceeded to the cafeteria, where the registration was taking place.

"Boy, I never saw so many runners before in one place," remarked Jeremy, "there must be five hundred here, at least."

"There will be more than this," added Phil, "these are just the early birds."

At the registration table, they both received their numbers after filling out the registration form and paying the twenty dollar entry fee.

Phil was in the 40-49 age group, while Jeremy was in the 50-59 division. There were awards given to the first three finishers in each age category, as well as to the overall male and female winners. The race even had an 80+ age group.

Since it was Jeremy's first road race, he decided to get near the rear of the pack of runners as everyone began to line up for the start of the race. While waiting, he couldn't help notice how diverse the runners were. They were young and old, tall and short, thin and heavy, as well as those who were very fit. Some were talking while others were just quietly standing there. A number of them were doing some last minute stretching exercises. All of a sudden, to Jeremy's surprise, the Star Spangled Banner was sung by a young woman with a beautiful voice.

When the gun was fired to start the race, the front runners took off like 'gazelles' and in a matter of minutes were far ahead of the rest of the pack. At the first mile marker, the runners' times were called out as they went by. When Jeremy heard his time, he was quite surprised to find out his time was a minute faster than what he had been doing on the track. He thought to himself *maybe I should speed up my pace a bit more. Perhaps, I can start passing some of these people I've been staying with since the race started.* To his amazement, Jeremy began easily moving ahead of some of the back of the pack runners.

Before he realized it, he had reached the two mile marker and heard his time called at an even twenty minutes. *I'm doing a ten minute pace,* thinking to himself, *if I keep this up I might finish the race in thirty two minutes.* Jeremy was feeling pretty good about his performance in his first road race.

As the runners raced along, one of them alongside Jeremy asked him, "How old are you?"

"I'm fifty five," he answered trying to catch his breath. This was the first time Jeremy had talked out loud since the race began.

"Gosh, you're doing great!" the other runner said, "do you run this race every year?"

"This is my first road race ever, how about you?"

"I've been running this race since it began ten years ago. I usually run about fifty races a year, but this is my favorite one. The refreshments they serve afterwards are better than most other races I run," remarked the other runner, "by the way, my name is Bart, what's yours?"

"Jeremy," came the reply.

"The finish line is coming up, Jeremy. I'll see you at the awards ceremony, O.K.?" Bart said as he sped off.

As Jeremy crossed the finish line, Geraldine was waiting for him in the large crowd that had lined up on both sides of the finish line chutes. Everyone was clapping and cheering aloud as each runner came in. Some finished the race looking like they could run many more miles, while some others looked as if they couldn't run another step.

Geraldine asked Jeremy, "How do you feel?"

"I feel great. I'm glad you decided to come, I wasn't sure you were going to make it. You know, my time was much better than what I was doing on the track. I guess the competition helps you to run faster."

While Jeremy and his wife were waiting in the refreshment line, they started up a conversation with the couple in front of them.

"What are your names?" Geraldine inquired, after exchanging pleasantries.

"We're the Moynihans," the wife responded, "Jim and Marie."

"And we are the Hamptons," answered Geraldine, "Jeremy and Geraldine."

"Do you race often, Jim?" inquired Jeremy.

"I enter about thirty races a year," responded Jim, "Marie races also, but she didn't run today, as you can tell by the way she's dressed."

"How often do you race, Jeremy?" asked Jim.

"This is my first, but I have a feeling I'll be doing a lot more. I really enjoyed the competition."

After they finished their refreshments, the two couples headed inside the school for the award ceremony. Trophies were given not only to the overall male and female winners, but also, to the top three finishers in each age division. When the names of the 50-59 age group winners were announced, Jeremy heard his name called as having won third place. He was completely surprised by this.

"I don't believe it," he said as he headed for his trophy, "my first race and I win something!"

Those in attendance gave Jeremy a nice round of applause as he posed for a picture with the race director and his assistant.

"Nice job!" the director said quietly, as he shook Jeremy's hand, "I hope you'll be back next year."

You bet I will," responded Jeremy.

While driving home after the race, Jeremy said to his wife, "I really enjoyed today's event. When you think about it, I never ran three miles before today. Maybe I'll train for a 10K race."

"Perhaps you should enter a few more 5Ks before taking on a longer one," Geraldine quickly added.

"I guess you're right, I could injure myself by doing too much too soon."

Chapter Two

Jeremy worked as a software engineer consultant and traveled quite a bit throughout the country. Every once in awhile, he would entertain thoughts of an early retirement, but he enjoyed his work too much to do that. Besides, he had two children in college, so retirement wasn't an option yet.

Since Jeremy had to take a business trip in a couple of weeks, he thought he'd get in touch with Phil to find out if there were any races coming up soon. He called Phil on the telephone and found out there was one on Saturday. Phil told him he'd do the driving.

While they were driving to the race, Jeremy noticed a couple of running magazines in the front seat beside him and began looking through one of them. Phil said to him, "I've finished reading those magazines, would you like to have them?

"Sure," said Jeremy, "there seems to be a lot of interesting articles in them. I also saw a list of races coming up that are being held all over the USA. I would be interested in checking out whether there are any being held in places that I frequent on my job. It would be fun to enter races in different parts of the country."

"I take it you travel a lot?"

"Yes I do. I used to hang around the hotels after work with little to do. Now, I'll be able to spend some of that time road racing or, at least, running to keep in shape. That might make my trips more interesting."

As they drove into the parking lot of the Fireman's Union building, Jeremy spotted Jim and Marie Moynihan. After the car was parked, Phil and Jeremy made their way to the registration table inside the building. Before they got there, Jeremy again saw the Moynihans and went over to speak with them with Phil following behind.

"Hi there, how are you both doing?" asked Jeremy.

"Very well," answered Jim, "we're glad to see you could make another race so soon after your first one."

"Thanks, I'd like you both to meet my friend, Phil," Jeremy said boastfully, "he is the one who introduced me to road racing."

"Glad to meet you, Phil," Jim and Marie said in unison.

"Nice to meet you both," responded Phil graciously.

"After we all get registered, why don't we run around the parking lot and warm up?" suggested Phil.

"Marie and I would like to do some stretching first, would you like to join us?" Jim asked.

"Sounds like a good idea, would you like to do some stretching, Phil" asked Jeremy.

"I'm all for it."

The foursome did their stretching exercises and then began to run around the parking lot for a warm up. A little later, they heard the announcement over the loudspeaker that it was time for the runners to line up for the start of the race. Jeremy noticed that Jim, Marie and Phil headed toward the middle of the pack of runners, so he decided he would join them there instead of going toward the rear. He felt a little more confident now that he had one race under his belt.

When the gun went off and the runners began moving out, Jeremy thought he would try to keep up with his new friends. He stayed with them for the first mile, but then Phil and Jim pulled ahead, while Marie and Jeremy kept about the same pace.

Jeremy was pleasantly surprised at his first mile time of 9:39. It was his fastest pace for a mile so far in his short racing career. Marie turned to him and said, "My usual time for a 5K is around twenty nine minutes or so. If you can stay with me, we both might equal that time. How does that sound to you?"

"That would be three minutes faster than my time in last week's race," Jeremy said hopefully, "I'll try my darndest to stay with you, Marie. So far, I've been able to. I wonder how Jim and Phil are doing?"

"Jim seems to always stay with me for the first mile, then he picks up his pace after that. He normally ends up in a 5K with a time just under twenty six minutes, he's usually happy with that."

"Maybe I'll be able to compete with Jim after I have done more racing, but that might take longer than I think."

"Don't forget, Jim is ten years younger than you and that can make a big difference."

"I suppose you are right, Marie, but I've always been a competitor. I thrive on competition. I've always been that way, no matter what I do. What I like about road racing is you can compete against people of all ages. That isn't possible in most other sports. That's why I know I'm going to enjoy racing," said Jeremy convincingly.

"Jeremy, you look like you've been holding back just to stay with me. If you want to speed up a bit, give it a try."

"O.K., Marie, I'll leave you now and, unless you catch up to me, I'll see you at the finish line," Jeremy said as he took off with a faster pace.

"Good luck, Jeremy!"

As Jeremy passed the two mile marker, he heard his time called out as 18:58. He thought to himself *if I can get to mile three in another nine minutes, I should be in real good shape.* While he was running along, Jeremy caught sight of Phil about a hundred yards ahead of him. He knew Phil was a much faster runner than he, so he reasoned something must have happened to him. As he caught up to him, Jeremy asked, "Are you having a problem, Phil?"

"Yeah, my hamstring is acting up again. Every so often this happens to me and I have to slow down my pace. I was doing real well, too, 'til the two mile mark," remarked Phil with much disappointment in his voice.

"Is there anything I can do for you?"

"No, thanks, I'll be O.K. You go ahead and I'll see you at the finish line."

"Alright, but just take it easy. We're almost at the end."

Jeremy crossed the finish line in a time of 28:32, a PR for him. Phil hobbled in with the time clock showing 29:20, while Marie arrived a few seconds later with a 29:27.

"How do you feel, Phil?" asked Jeremy looking at his leg.

"I'm O.K. I'll put some ice on the leg when I get home. That usually helps the hamstring when I do that."

After having refreshments and waiting for the last runner to come in, all the runners congregated inside a large room in the building for the award ceremony and the distribution of prizes. The runners' race numbers would be picked out of a bowl and whoever had their number called, would be able to choose one of the prizes that had been laid out on a table. All of the prizes were donations from local merchants and businesses in the area. Much to his surprise, Jeremy's number was called out, so he went to the table and picked out a Bill Rodger's book on running.

After all the prizes were gone, the awards ceremony began. Jeremy won third place again in his division. Jim came in sixth place in the 40-49 age group with a time of 25:10. Phil's time put him much farther down the list than he ordinarily would be, and Marie placed fourth in her division. The third place finisher beat her by three seconds, even though Marie had been ahead of her the entire race until the very end.

While walking to the parking lot, after the awards were all given out, Jeremy suggested, "why don't we all go out for dinner some evening?"

"Great idea," said Jim, "Marie and I like Christos."

"That's one of our favorite restaurants, too," Phil interjected, "my wife, Kathy, loves the lamb there. Maybe we can make plans after next Saturday's race, if we're all going to it."

"We are pre-registered for that one," said Jim, "how about you, Jeremy, can you make that race?"

"You bet. At the registration table, I picked up a flyer. I noticed that monetary prizes are awarded at that race to the top five finishers overall. I didn't think you could win money at races."

"There aren't too many that have that,' Phil remarked, "but it does tend to draw some pretty elite runners, when there is money on the line."

The four of them said their good byes and drove off for their homes with the understanding that they would meet the following Saturday and go out for dinner that evening. As Phil was dropping off Jeremy at his house, they both agreed they would be in touch sometime during the week.

After Jeremy got in the house, his wife told him that his boss wanted to talk to him right away. He did this and found out that he needed to fly out to the company's Colorado plant in order to straighten out some computer problems they were having out there.

"I hope I'll be back for next Saturday's race," exclaimed Jeremy to Geraldine.

"I haven't had the chance to tell you yet that at the race today we made plans to go out to dinner on Saturday evening. Phil will bring his wife and Jim and Marie were all in favor of it."

"That sounds like real fun, where were they thinking about going?"

"Christos, you have always enjoyed going there, right?"

"Absolutely," exclaimed Geraldine.

Chapter Three

On Monday, Jeremy took an early morning flight out of Boston to Denver, Colorado and arrived at the company's newest plant around 11:00 A.M. When he was told what the problem was, he knew it was going to take a few days to get the computer program back online. Jeremy went right to work on the project and was still at it until 9:00 P.M. By then, he decided to call it a night and went to his hotel where he had a late dinner.

The next morning, Jeremy thought he'd like to go out for a short run before breakfast. After running about a hundred yards, he stopped and tried to catch his breath. He couldn't understand what was happening to him. He thought to himself *I'm supposed to be in good shape, why am I breathing so heavily?* He decided to return to the hotel and get ready for work.

While at breakfast, he happened to mention what he experienced earlier to his waiter, who said, "don't you know you're a mile above sea level up here in Denver? The air is much thinner here and it takes a long time to get used to it. I'm a runner and it took me six months to get comfortable running in this altitude. I used to live in Florida, where it's mostly flat everywhere in the state."

"I guess I'll appreciate running at home more now after what I experienced this morning," said Jeremy to the waiter.

After breakfast, Jeremy reported for his second day of resolving the programming failure at his company's plant. He met with a small group of computer programmers and after consulting with them for a couple of hours, Jeremy had a pretty good idea where the problem was. By mid-afternoon, he found the solution and everything was back in working order. That evening, as a way of thanking Jeremy for his expertise and skillful handling of this dire situation, the Director of Operations and a few programmers treated him to a fantastic dinner at one of Denver's finest restaurants.

The next morning, as he was flying back to Boston, the pilot announced they were heading into some heavy weather and all passengers should fasten their seat belts. All of a sudden, there was a lot of thunder and lightning and the plane was being buffeted by extremely strong winds. Jeremy turned to the passenger next to him and said, "This is the most turbulence I've seen in all my years of flying."

The other man replied, "Would you believe this is my first flight since I was in a plane crash three years ago? I swore I'd never fly again and look what I'm facing now!"

"Where did that crash occur and were you seriously hurt?"

"What actually happened, the plane skidded off the icy runway at Dulles Airport and ended up on the highway after crashing through a fence. That scared the bejeepers out of me, but fortunately, no one was injured; just a lot of frayed nerves," said the man as he recalled the event.

As they were talking, they could feel the plane ascending. The pilot announced he was trying to climb above the storm and that proved to be the correct thing to do. In a relatively short period of time, the ride was once again smooth and steady.

"I'm glad that's over," Jeremy said with a sigh of relief.

"Our pilot did a great job getting us out of that situation," commented the other passenger.

"By the way, what's your name?" Jeremy asked.

"You can call me Ray," he responded, "what's yours?"

"I'm Jeremy, what's your business?"

"I work for Robox as a running shoe designer," answered Ray, "what is your line of work?"

"I'm a software engineer consultant, specializing in computer programming. I just left Denver on an assignment. I'm really interested in what you do, since I just began a new avocation, road racing. Maybe, you could advise me on a running shoe that would help me run faster, if such a thing exists."

"It's funny you should mention that! I've been working on a shoe that will give you a feeling that you're running on air. You'll hardly notice you're running on a hard surface. It's very heavily cushioned and it's called the Z-50. I've been developing this shoe for over a year now and the few runners that have tested it have given it rave reviews. We haven't put it on the market yet, we're still testing it with runners who work for the company. Would you like a pair to use in your races?" asked Ray.

"Are you kidding? This might be just the running shoe I need. I haven't been happy with the ones I have."

"When we land, I'll pull out a pair that fits you so you can try them out. I'll give you my card, so you can let me know what you think of them, O.K."

Upon arriving home late that afternoon, the first thing Jeremy did was put on his new running shoes and went outside for a short run. He couldn't believe how comfortable they felt and, as Ray had told him, he hardly felt the hard surface of the road. After his run, Jeremy went back to his house and Geraldine was waiting for him.

"I thought I heard a noise in the living room and when I came up from the basement, I saw your luggage, but didn't know where you were," she remarked with a surprised look on her face, "where did you go?"

"I had to try out my new Z-50 running shoes. I couldn't wait to see if they were what I was promised by a running shoe designer I met on the plane. I think I'll be able to run much faster with them."

"Not to change the topic, but how was your trip to Denver? Did you solve their problems?"

"Everything is back in tip-top shape and I'll have to tell you all about the trip over dinner tonight. I'm really excited about these running shoes. I'll have to give them a good tryout tomorrow morning and get in touch with Phil, also, about Saturday's road race. What's new with you? You look beautiful, as always!"

"Oh, thank you, it's good to have you home. It's lonely around here when you're gone."

"It's good to be home, Gerry, I missed you, too," said Jeremy as he gave his wife a big kiss.

At daybreak, Jeremy was on the road running with his newly acquired running shoes and heading for the track nearby. When he arrived there, he started his stopwatch since he likes to keep track of his times, both for the quarter miles and the miles that he runs. He records this in his running log book after every workout.

When he completed his first quarter mile, he checked his watch and couldn't believe his time of two minutes. *That's my best time for a quarter mile, since I started running,* he thought to himself, *it must be the new running shoes ,by golly!* At the half mile point, Jeremy again checked his watch, which showed four minutes. Again he thought, *if I keep up this pace I'll be able to do an eight minute mile. I haven't run this fast even in those races I was in.* Jeremy ended up running two miles on the track and managed to stay at the same pace the whole run. His time for the two miles was an even sixteen minutes and, needless to say, he was ecstatic! He could hardly wait for Saturday to come so he could try out his new running shoes in the race.

That evening Jeremy called Phil to discuss Saturday's arrangements and Phil told him he'd pick him up, as usual. Jeremy didn't want to mention his new running shoes to Phil until they got together, but he did tell Phil about his trip to Denver.

Chapter Four

On Saturday, Phil picked up Jeremy as planned. As they pulled into the school parking lot, Jim and Marie just happened to be right behind them, so they were able to find parking spaces right next to each other. After they said their hellos and exchanged pleasantries, Jim looked down at Jeremy's running shoes. "That's unusual looking footwear you have on, Jeremy. Where did you buy them?"

"Actually, they were given to me by a man I met who works for Robox."

"You haven't raced with them before, have you?" Marie asked.

"No, this will be the first time that I will have raced with them. I'm really anxious to find out if they'll make any difference."

After Phil and Jeremy registered, they went looking for Jim and Marie, who had pre-registered for today's race. They were already outside going through their stretching routine, when Phil spotted them as he and Jeremy went outside. They went over and joined them for some stretching before the four of them went for their warm-up run.

It was getting close to 10:00 A.M., the scheduled starting time for the race, when Phil suggested they better get in line before the gun went off. Jeremy, feeling pretty confident about his new shoes, decided to move closer to the starting line than he did the last race.

Jim said to him, "are you sure you want to be that close to the front, you're in the company of some really fast runners?"

"I'll be O.K., Jim. Those behind me can pass me whenever they wish. I feel I'll have a better chance to win my division if I line up here."

"Good luck, Jeremy," Jim said as the gun went off to start the race.

Jeremy felt real good running along and began to notice that not too many runners were passing him in the early stages of the race. He had his stopwatch going, so when he first looked at it, he saw a time of 7:30 and, at that moment, could hear a voice nearby shouting out times. *That must be the one mile mark coming up,* he thought and, sure enough, it was. As he passed the caller, he heard his time of seven minutes and forty seconds loud and clear. *Wow!* He thought, *that's almost two minutes faster than I did mile one in last week's race!* Jeremy actually found himself passing some of the other runners, which really boosted his confidence. As he passed the two mile marker, he heard the timer's voice shout out fifteen minutes. *My watch shows me I did that second mile in 7:20,* again thinking to himself, *if I can maintain this pace, I might finish with a PR of twenty minutes or so.* Jeremy crossed the finish line with a time of 22:45. He had beaten his previous 5K time by almost six minutes. Not only that, but he came in ahead of Jim, Phil and Marie.

Discussing the race later, while having refreshments, Phil said, "That was quite a performance you gave out there, Jeremy, I had you in my sights most of the way, but I couldn't catch up with you."

Then Jim piped in, "You ran a fantastic race, Jeremy, those running shoes must be very special!"

"You know, these running shoes were designed to add speed to any runner that uses them. You can't even buy them yet, but I might be able to get you all a pair. I'll call this afternoon and see what my friend Ray at Robox says and let you know at dinner tonight."

At the awards ceremony, Jeremy won his age division handily and won a fairly large trophy. When his time was announced, he received quite a loud cheer from the spectators there. For the next several minutes, he was surrounded by well-wishers. Jeremy was beginning to feel like a celebrity!

After the award ceremony was over, Jim, Marie, Phil and Jeremy got together to discuss dinner plans for that evening. The plan they decided on was that Jim and Marie, who own a seven passenger mini van, would do the driving and would pick up the others.

When Jeremy arrived home, Geraldine asked him, "How did you do with your new running shoes?"

"Would you believe it? I not only won my division, but I even beat Phil and Jim. I never thought I could run that fast! It had to be the shoes, wait 'til I tell Ray at Robox. Look at the size of the trophy I won!"

"I'm so happy for you, Jeremy, you must be thrilled beyond words!"

"I certainly am, and we're going to celebrate by dining out tonight. Jim and Marie will be picking us up at seven o'clock. and Phil and his wife are also coming. We haven't met her yet."

Later in the day, Jeremy called Ray and told him how much he liked his Z-50s and how well he did in the race today wearing them.

"Would you be willing to send me some of those shoes for three of my friends?" Jeremy asked.

"I'm afraid that wouldn't be possible, Jeremy," stated Ray apologetically, "we're still doing marketing research work on them. As a matter of fact, I was about to contact you to take part in our study. You are the only non-employee who has a pair of these shoes. Your input would be invaluable to us at this time. Would you be willing to participate in this research project?"

"I would be delighted to work with you and your company on this. What would you like me to do?"

"We would like you to come to our meeting on next Thursday. We'll be discussing a marketing plan for the Z-50. We might consider selecting a small number of runners to try them out. You may have some ideas on that aspect. The business card I gave you has our website on it, so you'll be able to pull up our Research and Development headquarters by visiting the site and getting the directions. The meeting is set for nine o'clock in the morning. Do you think you can make it?"

"I'll definitely be there, Ray, and thanks for the invitation."

That evening, the three couples dined at Christo's Restaurant and had a very pleasant evening together. They all had a chance to meet Phil's wife, Kathy, whom they had not met before. While at dinner, Jeremy announced to all what Ray from the Robox Company had offered him. Everybody had questions about the research project, but Jeremy had to tell them that he had few details to give them at the present time, but would have more information after Thursday's meeting. He told them he tried to get some more Z-50s, but was not successful.

"I'm going to try and persuade the research team to give me those shoes for Phil, Jim and Marie. I would be able to keep track of whatever results you three would experience running with them and, then, give the research team feedback. Maybe, they'll go along with that proposal, we'll see," said Jeremy.

"There's another race coming up on Saturday, Jeremy. You'll be able to fill us in at that time, if you are planning to compete on that day," suggested Jim.

"That's a great idea. I did plan on being in Saturday's race. That's the one with a lot of hills, isn't it?"

"It is," remarked Phil, "I've run that race many times. There's one hill just before the finish line that gives everyone trouble."

"I haven't done much hill work," Jeremy said, "I'll have to search out some steep inclines and forget about the track this week."

While the guys were talking about road racing, the gals were discussing other matters and getting to know each other better. It wasn't too obvious yet, but the three couples were forming a friendship that would be longstanding. They may have never met if Phil hadn't asked Jeremy to join him in that road race a short time ago.

Chapter Five

On Thursday, Jeremy drove over to the Robox R&D building and met with Ray and his research associates. Jeremy was shown how the Z-50 was developed and, also, talked with some company employees who had been using the new running shoe. The purpose of this meeting was to decide what the next step would be regarding marketing the new product. One proposal was for the sales staff to stock their various retail stores the usual way with some concentrated advertising beforehand. There were various opinions expressed about that type of marketing approach.

Another discussion centered around the selection of a certain location, even a small town, to see what kind of interest the shoes could generate there. As that proposal was being talked about, Jeremy raised his hand to be recognized.

"I have three friends, besides myself, who enter road races almost every weekend. If we were to wear the Z-50s at these races, we would be able to demonstrate to other runners what these running shoes are capable of doing for the average road runner. My time for the 5K race that I ran last Saturday was almost six minutes faster than the previous week's race. I can only attribute that to this phenomenal racing shoe. The proposal I would like to make would be for the Robox Company to publish a flyer advertising the Z-50s with a picture of the four of us wearing the shoes with quotations from us stating how our times improved dramatically the very first time we wore them. I'm sure the advertising department could put together something that would cause runners and even wannabe runners to want this merchandise. Naturally, we would need to race with the running shoes before the flyer was printed. I could bring them home with me today and the four of us could use them on Saturday. What do you think of that idea?" Jeremy asked.

"You know," Ray remarked, "I think your proposal has the makings of an excellent marketing program. Our research team will give this serious consideration and will consult with our Advertising Director, as well. I don't think we are ready to hand out those Z-50s just yet, but by next week we should have something definite to tell you. I will call you on Wednesday, Jeremy, O.K?"

"That is fine with me. Thank you all for giving me this opportunity to meet with you. I hope to see you soon," said Jeremy as he got ready to leave.

Jeremy left the meeting feeling fairly confident that what he said was well received. As he was driving home, he thought, *this would be fantastic if Robox gives my friends and me the opportunity to promote their product. Although, I must be cautious about raising their hopes too high, until I hear what the company definitely decides to do.*

On Saturday morning, Phil came by to pick up Jeremy and, of course, wanted to know how the meeting went. Jeremy said, "It went very well, but I won't know what decisions Robox will make until next week."

Before the race started, Jim and Marie asked Jeremy the same question that Phil did, and Jeremy had to give them the same response. When the gun went off, Jeremy started off strong with Phil, Jim and Marie behind him. Phil said to Jim, "I wonder if Jeremy realizes how tough this course is with three big hills in it!"

Jim's response was, "We'll find out if those shoes of his can help him glide over the steep inclines that we'll all be facing."

" The first one is coming up pretty soon, let's see how he does," Phil commented.

"He doesn't seem to be slowing down at all as far as I can tell! I think he's putting some distance between him and us. We might lose him in our sights, if we don't watch out."

Jeremy did pull away from his friends who never saw him again until they reached the finish line, where he was standing there waiting for them.

"Jeremy," Phil asked, "how did you make out on those hills? Did they slow you down at all?"

"You know, I can't believe I just sailed over them. It must be these phenomenal shoes. I even beat last week's time and, as I'm sure you remember, there were no hills in that race."

"I certainly hope you can get us a pair of those Z-50s," Jim said to Jeremy wishfully, "I wonder what they could do for us!"

Well, I should have an answer for you, one way or another, by next week, perhaps even before we race again."

"We'll be waiting to hear from you, Jeremy," Phil, Jim and Marie chimed in, as they all headed for the refreshments.

Later on at the award ceremony, Jeremy received first place in his division. As he was being handed the trophy, the race director announced over the microphone, "Jeremy has just established a new race record for his age division with a time of twenty two minutes." Those in attendance gave him a rousing cheer. As he headed back to join his friends, Jim said, "congratulations, Jeremy, if you keep this up you're going to have to get a trophy case."

While driving home from the race, Phil suggested, "Maybe we should get our wives to join us at these weekly races. If you could ask Ray at Robox for a couple of extra Z-50s, that might be enough to entice them.

"That's a great suggestion," said Jeremy, "we'll have to ask them when we get home. Let me know before Wednesday if Kathy is interested, O.K.?"

Upon his arrival home, Jeremy showed his newly acquired trophy to Geraldine, who remarked, "congratulations, you do nothing but win with those new running shoes."

"You might be a winner, too, if you had a pair. Would you like me to see if I can get some shoes for you when I talk to Ray on Wednesday?"

"You know, I have been wondering how I would do if I could try them out. After all, I was on the cross country team in high school. I used to love those races."

That afternoon, Phil called Jeremy to tell him that Kathy would be interested in getting a pair of the Z-50s, if the company were willing to do it.

Chapter Six

On Wednesday, as he promised, Ray called Jeremy on the telephone and told him that the research team had considered his proposal and thought it sounded like a great idea.

"I will send you three pairs of shoes for your friends, as you requested. After the four of you have raced with them several times, I want you to call and tell me how much of a difference the Z-50s made in your overall performances. In the meantime, I'll need to know the shoe sizes of your friends, O.K."

"That is fantastic news," replied Jeremy, "my friends are dying to hear what your decision was going to be. They'll be thrilled! Incidentally, would you consider two extra pairs of shoes for my wife and my friend's wife? We would then be a team of three couples entering the local races."

"That should be no problem, Jeremy. In fact, it sounds like your idea of a flyer with your pictures on it, would be greatly enhanced with the appearance of three couples. By the way, you might want to drive down and pick these shoes up before Saturday, if there is a race that day," suggested Ray.

"That's a good idea," said Jeremy, "I can drive down tomorrow and bring the shoe sizes with me. That will give the others a chance to get a practice run in before Saturday's race."

That evening, Jeremy called Phil and Jim to give them the good news. Needless to say, they were overjoyed with what he told them.

He asked them for shoe sizes and told them he would be picking up the shoes tomorrow.

On Thursday, Jeremy had all the shoe sizes from everyone and drove to Robox to get the Z-50s. He returned home right away and dropped them off at pre-arranged hiding places, since the other two couples were at work.

After dinner, Jeremy called his friends and asked them if they would like to join him and his wife at the nearby track so they could try out the new shoes. In no time at all, it seemed, all three couples were running around the track. Phil, Jim and Jeremy ran side by side with Marie somewhat behind. Kathy and Geraldine were further back.

Phil commented, "I can't believe how comfortable these shoes are. I can hardly feel the hard surface as my feet hit the pavement."

Jim was quick to add, "These running shoes are going to make a big difference in the way I run from now on, I can just feel it."

"I wonder how the gals are doing back there?" asked Jeremy, "Kathy and Gerry have not run for a long time. They'll have to decide if they need more time to train for the upcoming races."

Meanwhile, Kathy and Geraldine were chatting away while jogging. At one point, Geraldine said to Kathy, "Don't you just love these new running shoes?

Aren't they great?"

Kathy answered, "I really like them. I feel I could run much faster than I am. Do you want to pick up the pace a bit?"

"Let's do that. Maybe we can catch our husbands."

In no time, they passed Marie and pulled just ahead of the three guys. Not to be undone, the men decided to pass the women and were determined to stay ahead. In the meantime, Marie pulled alongside Kathy and Geraldine. After about fifteen minutes of running, they all decided to stop and talk about the workout.

Jeremy asked the group, "Well, what do think of the Z-50s? Aren't they something?"

Jim was the first to respond saying, "I think I could win my division with this fabulous footwear."

Phil responded to that comment saying, "You will have to beat me first."

Jeremy asked Geraldine and Kathy if they thought they would be able to run the race on Saturday, to which Kathy replied, "We can walk faster with these shoes, even if we don't run the whole way."

Marie gave her input with the comment, "I have never won in my age group, but I bet the Z-50s will help me do that."

They all decided to come back on Friday after dinner for another workout. They mainly wanted to break in the shoes before the race on Saturday. Racing with brand new shoes could cause blisters and no one wanted that.

Chapter Seven

The day of the race was a beautiful, sunny spring morning. The three couples arrived early for the event and were most eager to test their new racing shoes for the first time. Jeremy had high hopes that this entire 'project' of his was going to be highly successful. If the six of them did real well in this race, it would prove that this 'wonder' shoe was no fluke.

Once the race began, Jeremy, Phil and Jim ran together at a very fast pace. Normally, Phil and Jim could beat Jeremy when all three of them ran with ordinary running shoes, but Jeremy had already shown them he could beat them when only he had the advantage of the Z-50. Today it was a different story with all of them wearing the special shoes. They stayed together for the entire race until the last hundred yards, when Phil and Jim tried to make a mad dash for the finish line. Phil came in one second ahead of Jim and Jeremy crossed the finish line about twenty seconds later. Phil and Jim established new PRs for the 5K, while Jeremy's time equaled what he had done last week on the hilly course. Meanwhile, the wives were still engaged in the race. Marie came in about five minutes after the guys and set her own PR for a 5K race.

Finally, Kathy and Geraldine crossed the finish line admitting to their group that they had to do a certain amount of walking. After all, it was their first race since high school. They both felt pretty good for what they accomplished. Both agreed that they could not have finished the race without the special shoes.

After they enjoyed the refreshments, the three couples went over to the award ceremony, where they discovered that Jim won first place in the 40-49 age group and Phil won second place. Jeremy won his division and Marie came in first in hers. Kathy and Geraldine didn't expect to win and, of course, they didn't, not this time anyway.

On the drive home, Jeremy said to the group, "I haven't told you about the entire proposal I made to the Robox Company, have I?"

"What was it?" Jim asked.

"If we improve our race times considerably with the use of the Z-50s, Robox will have our pictures on their flyer advertising the benefits of the new racing shoe. In addition, our comments about our experiences with the shoe will be part of the ad as well. Does this sound like something you all would be willing to do?" asked Jeremy.

Marie quickly replied, "I think it's a super idea, Jeremy, I presume we will wear our regular running clothes."

"Definitely," said Jeremy, "I am sure the company will want a full picture of us showing our shoes, especially."

"When will this take place?" Phil asked.

"They said in about a month's time. We'll have to race every week before the month is up."

"We'll have to think of what we're going to say, won't we?" asked Kathy.

"After you race with these Z-50s a few times, you will know exactly what to say," Jeremy said assuredly, "we are almost home, so Gerry and I will see you at next week's race, O.K?"

"I will pick everybody up again on Saturday," said Jim.

Chapter Eight

It was toward the end of April when the three couples had completed enough races to satisfy the Robox Company's trial period to test the Z-50s. Everyone, including Kathy and Geraldine, felt the shoes boosted their road racing times considerably. In their most recent race, they all placed either first or second in their age group divisions. Jeremy's race times established a new record for his age division in his last four races. Phil and Jim set new record times in their age division, as well. It was time to have Robox take their pictures.

After Jeremy called Ray to tell him the group was ready for the next step, Ray suggested, "It might be much easier if I send our photographer to meet with the three couples, rather than you all having to come here. He could come some early evening, since some of you have day jobs. How does that sound to you, Jeremy?"

"That's an excellent suggestion, Ray. We could pose for the picture on the track that we use. When would you want our comments about the Z-50s?"

"You could give them to the photographer and then we'll send them to our ad department. I will have George, our photographer, call you tomorrow, O.K.?"

"Fine," said Jeremy, "I'll let everyone know what's going to happen."

George came around mid-week and took a lot of pictures. He arranged everyone in a variety of poses. There were pictures taken of individuals, couples and the whole group. They all wore their running clothes and, of course, their Z-50s. Before George left, Jeremy gave him an envelope with the various statements from each member of the group. Some had written a whole page about what the new shoe did for them. The guys wrote briefer commentaries than the gals, but they knew the ad department would sort all that out.

In a few days time, Ray called Jeremy to let him know the advertising department was working on the flyer and that everything was moving forward really well.

"We will send you out a proof next week before the flyer goes to the printing department; it is crucial that your friends see this and critique it. We don't want any of you unhappy with something that will be circulating the entire country. My feeling is that all of you will be thrilled when you see it."

"From what I have experienced so far with your company, I am sure we will," exclaimed Jeremy, "I'll be looking forward to receiving the proofs."

The proofs arrived on Saturday and, since there was no race nearby, Jeremy invited everyone to look at the proofs and make any suggestions they might have. There were copies for each one and, so, they spent a couple of hours examining every aspect of the proofs. No one could find anything that displeased them. In fact, as a whole, the group thought everything looked better than they imagined it would.

"You say the flyer will be distributed all over the country?" Marie asked.

"That's right," said Jeremy, "so you may be getting phone calls from people you haven't heard from in years, if they recognize your picture."

"At least, our last names don't appear," Kathy remarked.

"I had written almost a whole page of comments," Geraldine said, "and they boiled it down to a nice concise statement. I like it."

Chapter Nine

In a few weeks time, the Robox Company began the circulation of its flyer throughout the USA. Runners of all ages were flocking to stores buying the Z-50s so fast that Robox had to establish a third shift just to help meet the demand.

On the Saturday following the distribution of the flyers, Jeremy, Geraldine and the other two couples were registering for a race, when they noticed quite a number of runners wearing the Z-50 racing shoes. Some of the runners recognized the three couples whose pictures they had seen on the flyer and came up to them with all kinds of questions.

One of them asked Jeremy, "Are these shoes really as good as you stated in the flyer?"

Jeremy said to him quite assuredly, "You will be amazed at how much faster you can run with them. Talk to me after the race and tell me how you did, O.K.?"

Several others gathered around the three couples as word spread around the large room that the people in the flyer were here. The three couples were becoming a bit embarrassed by all the attention directed toward them. Finally, Jeremy said to his group, "We better get outside and do some stretching before our warm-up run."

As the runners began to line up for the start of the race, the three couples couldn't seem to escape all the attention others were paying to them. They finally got a break when the gun went off.

This race was so different from the most recent races that Jeremy and the others had been in because then they were the only ones wearing the special shoes. Today they were competing with many who also had them. This was slated to be a very interesting race, to be sure.

As Jeremy was running along the race route, he thought to himself, *I'm wondering if this was such a good idea with all these competitors wearing the Z-50s. At least, many runners are going to be very pleased with their performances.* Jeremy could see the smiles on the faces of those wearing the 'wonder' shoes.

At the award ceremony, there were trophies won by runners who never thought they'd ever win one. Jeremy did win his age division, Jim and Phil came in second and third respectively, while the gals did well, but didn't win in their age groups.

The race director, knowing the three couples were pictured in the flyer, invited them on the stage and announced to all who they were. The crowd gave them a resounding applause. Jeremy and the others in his group began feeling like celebrities. They weren't sure they were ready for all this attention.

On the ride home, Jeremy asked the group, "What did you think of today's race?"

Marie's response was, "I never expected that so many would recognize us! It was overwhelming!"

"You're right," said Kathy, "and I feel the majority of the well-wishers were trying to thank us for making them aware of this racing shoe that is going to be the rage of the running world."

"There was some fierce competition out there today," Jim added, "I couldn't catch the fellow that beat me for first place in our age group. He was really flying with his Z-50s on. I talked to him later and he thanked me for being the reason why he bought the shoes. He told me my statement in the flyer convinced him to do it. I felt pretty good hearing him say that."

"I'll have to contact Ray at Robox and tell him about our experiences today," said Jeremy, "he will be pleased to hear that there were so many runners wearing the Z-50s. If that were any indication, these shoes must be selling like hotcakes right across the country."

On Monday morning, Jeremy made his call to Ray and filled him in with everything that occurred at Saturday's race. Needless to say, Ray was very pleased to hear this input.

"It would be nice to know what the reaction is from other runners around the country," Ray interjected, "We know the Z-50's sales are better than we ever expected, but we would be very interested in hearing what runners are actually saying about them."

"Maybe you should have a person contact race directors nationwide and have them distribute a questionnaire that would ask runners to write down their answers to specific questions about the Z-50s. I could prepare something along that line for the next race I'll be in, just to test how runners receive this," suggested Jeremy.

"I like that idea," said Ray, "why don't you try a questionnaire and see what you come up with and then get back to me."

Later that day, Jeremy called the race director of the race being held the following Saturday and asked if he could announce at the award ceremony that he had a questionnaire for those runners who were wearing the Z-50 racing shoe. The race director, who already was aware of these shoes, gave his whole hearted approval.

At the award ceremony, after the race on Saturday, Jeremy made his announcement and the response was tremendous. More runners had the shoes at this week's race than last week. Every one of them filled out a questionnaire and handed them in before they left the building.

That afternoon, Jeremy and Geraldine read over each form and were delighted at what the runners had written down. In the comment section, they found very many positive statements. A number of respondents wrote that they were going to buy a second pair of Z-50s just in case the demand exceeded the supply. After having read them all, Jeremy put them in a large envelope and mailed them to Ray at Robox. A few days later, Ray called Jeremy to tell him that he had received the questionnaires.

"It looks like the runners in your area are quite pleased with the Z-50s," said Ray, "it would be nice to know how runners in other parts of the country are reacting to them."

"I could try to contact more race directors in my general area, but I don't know if I will have time to do that right away. I have some business in Nebraska next week and in California the week after that," explained Jeremy.

"We have people who can devote time to getting in touch with race directors. If you don't mind we would like to reproduce your questionnaire so it can be distributed nationally. Is that O.K. with you, Jeremy?" asked Ray.

"That is fine with me, Ray. I hope the responses will be as good as what we had."

"You know, Jeremy," said Ray, "when you get back from California, I would like you to come to our main office and spend some time discussing this whole Z-50 project with me. After all, you have played an integral part in the promotional campaign of our newest product and are due some well-deserved recognition. Please call me when you get back home, O.K.?"

" I will definitely do that, Ray."

Chapter Ten

When Jeremy returned home from his West Coast trip, he called Ray to tell him he was available to meet with him. The next day Jeremy drove down for the meeting with Ray. It was at that time, Ray said something to Jeremy which caught him by surprise.

"You have been so instrumental in our Z-50 promotional campaign that we would like to put you in charge of our marketing department. How does that sound to you, Jeremy?"

"I am certainly honored to think your company would offer me such an important position. What happened to the man that is currently heading up that department?"

"He will be retiring to Florida in another month, so he would be available to go over the entire operation with you, if you are interested."

"I am very interested, but I would need to talk to my company and to my wife before I can give you my answer."

"I'll be waiting to hear from you, Jeremy, have a safe trip home."

When Jeremy arrived home, he told Geraldine about his meeting with Ray and the job offer made to him.

His wife asked, "Do you think you want to leave the company you have been with for so many years and take on a whole new responsibility?"

"You know I gave a lot of thought to that while I was driving home. I guess what makes me so interested in the position is that I like the work ethic of all the people I have met at Robox. I also would be involved with any new products they develop in the near future. Ray did mention sneakers that he is designing for basketball players and special cleats for football players. These are exciting times at the company."

"I can see why you would be interested. Have you thought about what you will say to your boss?"

"Well, since I have only been a consultant for the company the last few years, I don't think I would cause too much hardship if I left."

After a week went by, Jeremy called Ray and told him he would happily accept the new position offered to him. Ray curiously asked, "How did your boss react to your decision?"

"He thought it was a perfect time for me to do this. I had kept him aware of my involvement with Robox. He wished me the best of luck in my new endeavor. I should be ready to start next Monday."

"That's great," replied Ray, "We will be expecting you and look forward to having you in our employ."

Chapter Eleven

Jeremy and the outgoing head of the marketing department worked well together as he began his new assignment. The department head's name was Charles and he gave Jeremy an excellent indoctrination into the workings of this vital part of the company. After a couple of weeks, Charles turned the reins over to Jeremy for good.

Once Jeremy was in charge of marketing, he made it a point to meet with Ray on a regular basis. Ray was an idea man and Jeremy would quiz him often about any new things he had in mind.

Ray had an idea for a new basketball sneaker with a special innersole and heel that allowed the user to leap a foot higher than any other one on the market. Like the Z-50, in its initial stages, this sneaker had only been tested in the company's gymnasium by some employees who were basketball enthusiasts.

"Gee, I would like to see these guys in action," Jeremy said to Ray.

"We can watch them at 3 P.M.. There will be several of them in the gym at that time."

Ray and Jeremy sat in the stands and watched the action. Jeremy could not believe how high each player could jump. A couple of them were quite small in stature and yet were able to touch the rim of the basket with little effort. Jeremy said to Ray, "This could change the basketball game forever. Big men would no longer have the advantage they now have."

"Don't forget the big men will be able to jump even higher as well."

"It should make the game very interesting, to say the least," Jeremy added.

"This sneaker is designed to be able to stop even on a wet floor, which often happens when sweaty bodies fall down."

"How are you planning to market this product?" Jeremy inquired.

"That is one of the reasons we hired you, Jeremy. Your thinking regarding the Z-50 was so innovative, we thought you would have some novel ideas for this project."

"Well, thank you for the compliment. I guess I'll have to give some thought to this. I would think every one that plays basketball would want this, wouldn't you?" asked Jeremy.

"You would think so, but there are always skeptics who need to be shown proof of a product before they buy."

"This could be a better seller than the Z-50!" said Jeremy optimistically, "I'm really excited about the possibilities."

For the next week, Jeremy was consumed with possible marketing ideas for the new product. He wondered if any professional team would be willing to try them out before their regular season began. He asked Ray what he thought about that approach and Ray was all in favor of it.

Jeremy sent out letters to all the professional basketball teams and the response was not too favorable. Only one team, the Connecticut Yankees, wrote back and said they would be interested in trying them out when they held their summer camp in a few weeks.

All the players who reported to camp were outfitted with the new sneaker, which by now was called the Climber, because it enabled the user to get off the floor higher. It was a huge success at the summer camp. The players could not believe how high they could jump with them. They were all able to do fancy maneuvers that they were never able to do before.

When it came time for the exhibition season to begin, the Yankees couldn't wait to show off their new footwear. Their first game was against a very good Illinois team and it wasn't even a contest. Connecticut outscored them 92 to 46. The Illinois players were astounded at what some of their opponents were able to do. The game was more like a college team playing a high school team; it was so lopsided.

After the game, the Illinois coach asked the Connecticut coach, "how come your players didn't play like that in the regular season last year when you had the poorest record of all the other teams in the entire league?"

"Since you are such a good friend of mine," the other coach said, "I'll let you in on a little secret. My players are wearing a newly developed sneaker that a company by the name of Robox makes. I am amazed at how my team's spirit, as well as their performance, has changed since they started wearing them. They were pretty disconsolate after last season ended. Now they are rarin' to go!"

"That must be the company that sent me some correspondence about a new sneaker and I just felt it couldn't be what they said. I've been around too long, but I guess I was wrong," admitted the Illinois coach, "maybe I should get in touch with Robox."

"I have a feeling these sneakers could revolutionize the game of basketball. Why don't we keep this secret to ourselves for awhile and see how your team does after you get a supply of them," suggested the Connecticut coach.

In a week or so, the Illinois coach ordered the Climber from Robox and the players wore them for the first time in an exhibition game against the Kansas Bulls. The players never got a chance to try them out in practice, so it took awhile to get used to them playing against an opponent. They did much better with them in the second half and won by forty points.

The Kansas coach met up with the Illinois coach after the game and started asking him the same kind of questions that had been asked of the Connecticut coach previously. Before long, the entire league began hearing about this super new sneaker and began putting in orders for them. Once all the players started wearing the Climber, it leveled the playing field, so to speak, and, as a result, there was much more parity in the league than ever before.

College and high school basketball coaches from all over the country were requesting the sneakers in record numbers, as word spread about them. Athletic directors were ordering the Climber for their intramural basketball programs. Thousands of youth organizations across the nation were raising funds in order to buy new sneakers for their members.

Meanwhile, Robox was doing their level best to keep up with the demand. Once again, the company needed to put on a third shift to keep up with the high volume of orders.

At a recent meeting with Ray, Jeremy said to him, "I don't know how you keep coming up with products that catch on so well; the Z-50 and now the Climber. When did you find out you had such an inventive mind," asked Jeremy.

"I have always enjoyed tinkering with things; as a young boy I was forever trying to make things out of ordinary household items that I would find around the house. I once made a contraption that converted paper clips into heavy duty wire. While a sophomore in high school for the annual science fair I developed a robot that monitored the school hallway. It would tell students to walk when a sensor inside the robot detected rapid motion nearby. I even entered the national high school science fair and won first prize with my invention. I was real proud of that."

Chapter Twelve

"What is the status of the football cleats you said you were designing?" Jeremy asked.

"I have made excellent progress with them. I have built a heating/cooling system into them so they can be adapted to all kinds of weather conditions. On a frigid December day, football players would relish wearing a shoe that was heated. The ones who would appreciate that feature the most would be those back-up players on the team who sit on the bench most of the game. Furthermore, players who are from cities in warmer climates would love to have a heated shoe when they travel north."

"What other features have you built into the shoe?"

"I have designed cleats that would be adapted for all kinds of weather. Football players play on fields that might be rain soaked, muddy or covered with snow. This football shoe can withstand the worst of field conditions. This might be the best product I have come up with so far. Players from the professional teams down to Pop Warner will crave this footwear, I'm certain."

"How are these going to be tested?"

"We have a large field adjacent to our Research and Development laboratory. We can create different weather related conditions there, and that is where we have been testing the football cleats. All our experimentation is done with employees who volunteer for the program. Come on down and I'll show you the operation."

"Do you think we could market this in the same way we did with the Climber," asked Jeremy as they made their way to the lab.

"Well, since you are the Director of Marketing, I'm going to lean on your expertise once again."

After observing the laboratory and the field next to it, Jeremy was very impressed with the entire facility. "We could invite the local Norton Community College to play their home games on this field," suggested Jeremy, "They are starting up a football program this coming fall season and have been looking for a field to host their games. We could outfit them with the new football cleats and have the opportunity to observe firsthand how the players perform with them."

"Fabulous suggestion, Jeremy! I knew we could count on you to come up with what could be a perfect solution for our new venture."

"I will contact the college tomorrow and see if they are interested in this arrangement. If they are, we'll have to consider erecting stands for the spectators, as well as lights and goal posts. Our laboratory has enough room in it to accommodate the teams at half time, from what I have observed."

Jeremy did get in touch with the community college and spoke with the athletic director, who asked if he and some others from the college could come over and inspect the premises, as well as the new football shoes that Jeremy had described to him. The very next day the athletic director and several administrators arrived in order to check everything out. Robox had several employees on hand to demonstrate what the football shoe could do in a weather controlled setting. A variety of field conditions were set up by the lab technicians to the amazement of the onlookers.

"It looks like those football cleats can adapt to all kinds of weather situations," remarked the astonished athletic director, "did you say our team would be the first one to ever use this type of footwear?"

"That is correct," Jeremy answered boastfully, "we are confident we have a superior product ready for the market, but we want to see how it stands up in real game situations. That is why we are offering it to your football team."

One of the college administrators asked, "do you plan to put up stands for our students and fans, as well as for the fans of the visiting teams?"

"Most assuredly," Jeremy replied, "we will erect lights and goal posts also. What do you people think of our proposition?"

The athletic director was the first to respond to Jeremy's question as he carefully chose his words, "this is a fantastic opportunity for our newly formed football program, but we will have to talk to our Board of Directors. They oversee all academic and non-academic programs and I believe they would approve what you are offering us without hesitation. We will just have to get back to you as quickly as possible."

"That's fine," said Jeremy, "we will be waiting to hear from you."

After about a week, the athletic director called Jeremy and said, " I want to let you know our Board of Directors did approve our going ahead with the plan you proposed. Just let us know when our players can come over to be outfitted with those football shoes."

"They can come anytime during the day. There is always someone at the lab that would accommodate them. While they are there, the players might want to see the lab equipment that causes the field to have a variety of weather related conditions. I am sure they will enjoy the inner workings of that operation. Just give us a call when they might be coming," Jeremy suggested.

"When could they try out the cleats on the field with the different conditions?" asked the A.D.

"They could use the field the day they come over for the shoes," explained Jeremy, "our lab people can prepare the field however you wish. It may seem strange to the players at first, but it will afford them an opportunity to try out the cleats that can handle every kind of condition. It will be interesting to observe how these players handle this experiment."

Over the next couple of months, the Robox Company had contractors come in to convert the field into a fully equipped football stadium with a seating capacity for ten thousand spectators. Fortunately, the area was large enough to make a huge parking lot adjacent to the stadium. The workers also installed a quarter mile track circumventing the football field. Unless there was a football game in progress, the track could be used by customers who bought the Z-50 running shoe and other footwear at the company's retail store. Many of the employees of the company could use the track as well.

Chapter Thirteen

The Norton Community College football team had their first scheduled game at home with Barton State College. As if it were meant to be, it rained the day before the game and, as a result, the field was very wet and slippery. While the Barton players had a terrible time keeping their footing during the game, the Norton players had no problem at all. They were not sliding or slipping and the Barton State players could not understand why they were having such difficulty and their opponents were not. Norton won the game 48-0 and the Barton players left the stadium shaking their heads in disbelief. They had won all but two of their games last season, and this year they suffer a loss to a brand new team.

The Norton players were ecstatic over their lopsided victory and knew that their special football cleats were the main reason they were able to keep from sliding around on the slippery surface.

After the game, Jeremy and Ray were heading out of the stadium and Jeremy asked him, "when do you think we should begin marketing our new product; after all, the football season is underway?"

"You know, Jeremy, I keep reminding you that you have to make the marketing decisions, now that you are the head of the marketing division."

"O.K.," interjected Jeremy, "why don't I invite some area coaches and athletic directors to come and observe the Norton players practice in the poor field conditions that our lab technicians can create. I know it is a busy time for them, now that the football season has begun, but my letter might be convincing enough to have them or a representative come to see what we have to offer. It certainly is worth a try and if that's not successful, we'll try another approach."

"That sounds excellent to me, Jeremy. Up to now your ideas have worked out superbly."

Shortly after Jeremy's letter was mailed out, a surprising number of responses came back from coaches and others who were intrigued by what they read regarding this unique football shoe that had so many special features. The majority of the respondents said they could come on the day Jeremy had stated in his letter, which was the first Tuesday in October at three o'clock in the afternoon.

One of the coaches asked if he could bring his team over for a scrimmage game against Norton on that afternoon. After that request was made, Jeremy checked with the Norton coach, who was in favor of it.

More people came to the field that Tuesday than Jeremy had expected. Some who received his letter decided to come without notifying him, while others brought extra people. It was not a problem, having too many attending the event, since there were all kinds of room in the stands.

During the scrimmage it was announced that the Norton team had the specially designed all weather football cleats, while the other team, which was from another community college, would be wearing conventional football shoes. Those in attendance were also informed that the field conditions would change in a variety of ways during this match between the two teams.

The lab technicians, on cue from Jeremy, could change the conditions on the playing field in a matter of minutes. Both teams knew what would be taking place and were ready for the action to begin.

The first change on the field was a frozen surface that made traction difficult for the visiting squad. The Norton players moved around with no trouble at all. This was very obvious to those watching from the stands and, little did they know, the show was just beginning.

The next thing the spectators witnessed was thick mud spreading all over the field. This was an amazing phenomenon to see since it was a sunny afternoon. Again the visitors could hardly keep their footing, while the Norton team played like they were on a dry field.

After two or more field condition changes, the visiting players decided they had enough and requested to have a dry field for the remainder of the scrimmage game. After their request was granted, neither team had an advantage, but the message was very clear to all observers and participants. The special football shoe proved what it could do, no matter how poor the condition of the field.

Knowing that there might be an immediate demand for this extraordinary footwear, Jeremy made an announcement over the loudspeaker that the shoes were available for purchase in the retail store next to the laboratory. As soon as he said this, there was a stream of people heading directly toward the store. Before long, the line circled around the entire lab building. Most of the buyers were people from athletic departments of various colleges and high schools in the general area. Since the retail store had only a limited supply on hand, orders had to be written up. The cost of these football shoes was $300 a pair, so there were a lot of credit cards being used that day.

After the exhibition scrimmage game ended, it didn't take long for word to disseminate that the Robox Company had come out with a unique football shoe to which only a few teams had access. The company immediately put ads on T.V., in newspapers and in magazines, in order to make consumers aware of their latest product and that it was available for all who wanted it.

Jeremy made certain that all the professional football teams knew of this all-weather shoe by sending them a smartly styled flyer illustrating the shoe's various features. These flyers were also mailed to every college and high school athletic department in the entire country.

As various teams received their orders and players began wearing the shoes in games, the demand for this remarkable footwear began to increase in ever increasing numbers. Once again, Robox needed to keep their third shift working in order to keep up with the volume of requests.

After a few weeks went by, letters came pouring in to Robox from everywhere extolling the fantastic features of the fabulous football shoe. Even some of the biggest stars among the pros sent thank you notes. One professional player, who had been in a hard fought game with the temperature in the nineties, wrote how the shoe's cooling element helped his whole body to cool down, even in the heat of battle, as he put it.

Chapter Fourteen

As Ray and Jeremy were having lunch together in the company cafeteria on one particular day, Ray said to Jeremy, "this has been quite a year for Robox. We have had great success with the Z-50, the Climber and now the all-weather football shoe for which no one has come up with a name yet. Maybe somebody will label it after it has been worn for awhile."

"You must be working on something new, now that your three latest successes have done so well."

"You may be surprised to hear this, but I am going to seek suggestions from people who are involved in all kinds of sporting endeavors. I'm sure there are many golfers, soccer players, rock climbers, skiers, cyclists, to name a few, who might have some ideas for their footwear that could improve their performances in whatever sporting event they participate. Look what we have done for the runners, as well as basketball and football players. We have revolutionized those sports. Maybe we can make sweeping changes in some others."

"How would you propose to contact such a vast amount of sporting enthusiasts?" asked Jeremy expecting to be challenged.

"Here we go again, Jeremy, you know you are the one I turn to when I need something publicized. I'll let you figure out something."

"I just thought of something that might reach many thousands of people," replied Jeremy, "as we advertise our products on T.V., we could ask viewers to write down any ideas they may have about their sport's footwear, even if it sounds impractical or impossible, and e-mail them to the company's website or mail them to our R&D address. What do you think of that idea?"

"I don't know how you do it, Jeremy, but you always seem to come up with clever suggestions for which I can only applaud you. We can visit the ad department after lunch to talk about your plan."

Once the commercials went on T.V., thousands of e-mails and letters flooded the company's computer network and mail room. Certain employees had to be taken away from their regular duties just in order to read all the mail and categorize it according to the sport being addressed. One writer wanted his soccer cleats to swivel so he could reverse himself more quickly. A rock climber wanted shoes that had spikes sharp enough to penetrate rock. A pole vaulter wrote hoping footwear could be developed that would enable him to clear the bar at twenty feet. There were so many requests that bordered on extreme fantasy, the readers of these letters found much humor in them.

Ray came across a letter that really caught his interest. It was from an eleven year old boy, by the name of Barry, who was overweight and was picked on because of it. He had tried to lose weight but was never successful. His letter requested if a shoe could be developed to help him, in some unrecognizable way, to lose weight. Ray wrote back to Barry and told him he was going to try and satisfy his request, but would like to meet with him first.

A short time later, the boy and his parents came to Robox and had a very nice visit with Ray, who took a real liking to the boy. Ray weighed him, measured his height and foot size and even observed at what pace Barry walked, which happened to be a very slow one. He also had him meet with the company's nutritionist. Ray informed the boy and his parents that he would need to come back periodically as the new shoe was being developed.

Ray's idea was to install a mechanism in the shoe that could trigger the feet to move so a person would be able to either walk or run faster and, thus, burn off more calories. He knew this was a shoe that would not only help Barry, but had the potential of helping other obese boys and girls, as well as adults of all ages, since obesity has become such a national problem.

After a few more shoe fittings with Barry, Ray felt he had his latest undertaking fully tested and ready to be worn. Since it was his summer vacation period, Barry was able to remain at the R&D complex for a couple of weeks. He had permission to bring his close friend, George, to stay with him for companionship, which was fine with Ray. George also had an obesity problem, so Ray decided to have both boys wear the special shoes during the experimental sessions that were planned. Of course, the parents of both boys were completely supportive of what Ray was doing, since they were very concerned about their sons' weight problems and self-esteem.

Ray's plan was to have the boys walk and run on the track three times a day with a weigh-in at the end of the last daily workout. Naturally, they wore headphones so they could listen to their favorite music.

In the shoe was a timer which was pre-set for fast walking for five minutes and running for two. The timer could be set for a variety of speeds and times for both walking and running. If it were left up to the two boys, they might set the times for slow speeds, but Ray was able to control the various speeds from a lab room that had a window facing the track. From there he could observe the boys and could actually communicate with them over their headphones.

The boys were happily enjoying this novel experimental program in which they were involved, but were seriously attempting to see positive results since they both had a similar problem of overweight. They would walk and run on the track as Ray controlled the timer settings. At the end of the day's third session, Ray asked the boys how they felt and they told him their legs were a little tired, but not that bad.

This series of walk/run exercises continued for the planned two week period and on the last day, the boys' parents were on hand to view the program in action. Barry's mother said to Ray unbelievingly, "Is that my son walking that fast and even running?"

"The boys have been most cooperative in this venture and, as a result, have made the experiment a complete success," Ray announced to both sets of parents.

"They look like they have lost weight," commented Barry's father.

"Indeed they have," Ray boasted, "in a few minutes they'll come over for a final weigh-in. You are all going to be pleased."

On Ray's signal, the boys came off the track and received big hugs from their parents. "Let's go to the scales," Barry said to his friend, "our parents are going to be quite surprised."

The final weigh-in showed Barry had lost fifteen pounds and George thirteen. Everyone was thrilled with the results. Ray's ingenuity had proven itself once again.

As the boys and their parents began to get ready to leave, they showered Ray with hugs and congratulatory comments. In parting, Ray said to the boys, "don't forget to use these shoes as you have been instructed and we'll all meet here two months from today."

Ray had been so busy with his new experiment and the ensuing time with the two young boys, he hadn't seen too much of Jeremy. They happened to bump into each other one noontime while both were heading for the company cafeteria.

"How did your new experiment go with the boys?" Jeremy asked.

"Everything went very well, Jeremy. I was about to contact you regarding marketing this new product. What do you think of the name Slimmer for it?"

"That has possibilities," was Jeremy's immediate reaction.

"With so much obesity in the country today, this shoe could make a difference," remarked Ray.

"Do you think people will know how to operate the timing devices in the shoe properly?" asked Jeremy.

"It shouldn't pose a problem. The instructions that will be in the shoe box are quite clear. Besides, the retail stores handling the sale of them will have to sign an agreement stating that all sales people will need to give a demonstration to each and every buyer."

"We will certainly want feedback from all those who purchase the shoe, since it is designed for the user to lose weight," said Jeremy, "and as we receive comments from buyers, with their written permission, we can pass on what they said to potential customers through our advertising circulars."

"What I like about this new product," said Ray, "Robox will be instrumental in helping the country combat a serious health problem. People of all ages, sizes and shapes will be able to wear this shoe and get as much from it as they put into it."

"That is well stated, Ray. Those very words could be put right in our ads. Sometimes I wonder who the marketing expert around here is, you or me!"

The Slimmer was advertised in magazines, newspapers, circulars and, of course, on T.V. Over the course of a few months some people wrote to the company overjoyed with the weight they had lost. Others wrote in telling about the various diets they had tried and had failed, but were experiencing definite weight losses because of the Slimmer. An unexpected large number of people paid tribute to Robox for merchandising footwear for people who were desperately searching for a solution to their obesity. Robox was even given the annual distinguished Conquer Obesity Award by the President's Fitness Council.

After awhile, the Slimmer took on a life of its own. Fund raising race events were being held here and there with some contestants wearing the Slimmer and others wearing ordinary walking or running shoes. The object of the race was to see if those with Slimmers could outwalk or outrun those without them. Different rules were made depending on who was putting on the event, but participants always enjoyed themselves and, at the same time, raised money for a worthy cause.

Chapter Fifteen

All the time that Jeremy had been the Director of Marketing, he commuted between his home and his workplace. It was a forty five minute drive each way and some nights he would arrive home quite late in the evening. He and Geraldine had been talking from time to time about selling the house and moving closer to his work , but they didn't talk about it seriously until Jeremy drove home this one particular night in a blinding snowstorm. It was a nightmarish commute with cars and trucks off the road and visibility down to about one hundred yards. When Jeremy arrived home that night, he said to Geraldine, whom he often called Gerry, "I hope I never have to drive again in weather like I did tonight. As soon as the good weather arrives, I think we should start looking at homes for sale in an area close to the Robox Company."

"Thank goodness you made it home safely," said Geraldine, "I was really worried about you. I think you are right, perhaps it would be a good idea to move closer to your job."

"I must give Phil a call one of these days," said Jeremy changing the subject, "ever since I got the job with Robox, he and I have only talked a couple of times. I wonder if he is still entering road races."

"We have lost contact with Jim and Marie, also," Geraldine added.

"I think I'll give both couples a call so we can go out to dinner some Saturday night," Jeremy said as he headed for the telephone.

Finally, a dinner engagement was made and the three couples got together. They had a lot to talk about since they hadn't seen each other for about six months. Jeremy was busy answering all the questions he was asked regarding his position at Robox. Everyone was quizzing him about the new products Robox had come up with and wanted to know what was next.

"You all have heard me speak of Ray," said Jeremy, "he is a remarkable individual. I don't know how he comes up with some of his ideas and then puts them into working order. I'm sure when I see him on Monday he'll be working on something new. Are you people still racing with your Z-50s?"

"Marie and I haven't done much this winter," said Jim, "but I remember some races late last fall, almost every runner had those Robox shoes on. Road racing has become more popular because of them. After races, all you would hear were people commenting on how well they did and how they established new PRs. Robox has been instrumental in changing road racing forever."

Phil remarked about the fact that he bought a pair of Climbers, since he belongs to a men's basketball league, and mentioned that everyone else was sporting a pair.

"There are more and more men wanting to join the league," he continued, "with the advent of these spectacular basketball sneakers. I couldn't believe what a difference they made in the way everyone plays the game. Some guys are slam dunking the ball now when, before the Climber appeared, they couldn't reach the rim. I'm seeing reverse jams and rebounding that I never used to see from most of the guys, whom I would call just ordinary jocks. It is a whole new game; a lot more fun. I guess you could say Robox changed basketball, also."

"Well, I'm hearing a lot of good news about my company," commented Jeremy, "I guess I made a smart move by accepting a position with them. My only regret is it has taken me away from our weekly races that I used to enjoy so much. Maybe in the spring, I'll enter some races with you."

"What if we move?" Geraldine interjected, "we will be further away from our friends."

"Are you two thinking of moving?" Kathy asked.

"We have been talking about it for quite some time," Jeremy replied, "after driving home in that snowstorm a week ago, I was convinced I should live closer to my work."

Jim's response was, "perhaps Ray could invent an all-weather car for you like his all-weather football shoe."

Everyone laughed at that comment as they all got ready to enjoy a nice dinner with good friends, who haven't been seeing each other as often as they would like.

Chapter Sixteen

On Monday, Jeremy had a scheduled meeting with the company CEO and the various department heads, to hear about a company, named Swim Works, that had fallen on hard times and was planning to go out of business. The products the company manufactured were swimming gear, floating paraphernalia, water safety devices and such. The purpose of the meeting was to decide if Robox should buy this company and forgo being just a company dealing with footwear.

"I would suggest, before making such an important decision," said Jeremy, "that some of us go over and visit the plant and see what the facility looks like."

The CEO asked if everyone was in agreement to Jeremy's suggestion and there was a unanimous show of hands.

After the meeting, Ray, Jeremy and some of the other executives visited the plant. They were met by Henry Taylor, the company president, who gave them a guided tour. As they were walking around, Henry wanted to know what plans Robox had for his ailing business.

Jeremy said to him, "all phases of the company would have to be examined by our department heads. We will need to look into your financial structure, your product line, your marketing history, just to name a few, before we decide to buy Swim Works."

"When did your company begin having problems?" asked Ray.

"Our products were not keeping up with the competition. We needed something innovative to boost sales, but it just didn't happen," explained Henry regretfully.

The head of the Production Department for Robox suggested, "I think it would be a good idea for both companies to have their respective department heads meet together as soon as it can be arranged. I'm sure a lot of useful information could come out of such a meeting."

"I am certain we can do that very soon," replied Henry, "you will find our people will be most cooperative."

Soon the plant tour ended with Henry shaking hands with all the Robox representatives.

About a month later the Robox executives met again and, having many more facts in hand, discussed the purchase of Swim Works. By the end of the meeting, it was unanimously agreed that Robox should make the purchase. One of the key reasons that convinced the managers to do this was Jeremy's touting of Ray's ingenious ability to transform ordinary objects into merchandise that consumers wanted. Everyone present was well aware of the contributions Ray had already made, which helped to reap huge profits for the company. Most of these same people had received healthy pay increases lately because of the great success Robox had been undergoing. Before the meeting broke up, Ray was given a hearty round of applause by his colleagues.

Ray stood up and said, "Thank you all for that kind recognition, but I needed all of you to bring about the final results of anything that I developed. Teamwork has been the key to our success. Let's keep it up."

About another month went by and all the paperwork that went along with the transfer of ownership was completed. Robox now owned Swim Works!

Not long after the takeover, Jeremy was having lunch with Ray and asked him, "have you given much thought to your next project?"

"I have several ideas regarding the products made by the company we just bought, but I seem to be narrowing it down to something that has to do with life jackets," answered Ray with an air of excitement in his voice, "I know there are a lot of people using boats of all kinds who can't be bothered wearing life jackets. Some people feel they are too cumbersome, others feel they are not necessary, and there are a lot of men, unfortunately, who are too macho to put them on."

"How would you change those attitudes, go on a lecture circuit?" asked Jeremy with a bit of sarcastic humor.

"No, wise guy. I have in mind a pocket sized life jacket."

"I know you have done some marvelous things so far, but this sounds like it is bordering on the absurd. I can't imagine how you could design and develop that," said Jeremy in disbelief.

"My plan would be to make a miniature life jacket that fits in your pocket or attaches to a bathing suit, so it would be with each person on a boat. All one would have to do to activate it would be to push a button and it would inflate itself to a regular size life jacket with straps. What do you think of that idea?"

"It could certainly save lives if a boat were sinking fast and people didn't have to go scrambling for their life jackets," answered Jeremy with more of an approving tone.

"That's when seconds count in an emergency boating incident. Even if one life were saved as a result of it, the device would be worth having. In fact I'm going to name it the Life Saver.

"When do you think you will have this ready for testing?" asked Jeremy with some newly gained enthusiasm in his question.

"I should have it in operation in a few weeks time. In the meantime you better start thinking about a good marketing approach. Can I count on you?"

"I'll get right on it. You can rest assured I'll do my level best."

On his long drive home late that afternoon, Jeremy had several thoughts going through his head regarding the Life Saver. He thought, *I could contact yacht clubs, cruise ship companies, sailing clubs, even the United States Navy and Coast Guard. I'll have to talk it over with Gerry at dinner tonight.*

While he and his wife were having their evening meal, Jeremy brought up the conversation he had with Ray and explained to her Ray's latest project. He put this question to Geraldine, "Whom do you think might be the biggest consumer of the Life Saver? Would it be the Navy, the Coast Guard, cruise ship companies or yacht clubs?"

"I would say, beyond a doubt, the Navy would be the biggest consumer, but like the Coast Guard, the government would need to get involved and that might take a long time to cut through all the red tape. My first choice would be contacting cruise ship companies. Remember the cruise we went on two years ago? That ship had thirty five hundred passengers and we had one evacuation drill as we lined up in front of those big bins holding the life jackets. The Life Saver could be carried around so easily on one's person that it wouldn't even be noticed. I think Ray has a fantastic idea. I hope he can make it work," remarked Geraldine wishfully as she crossed her fingers.

"Well, I guess you convinced me. I will get a directory of cruise ship companies and get to work on it as soon as Ray completes the testing phase of the Life Saver."

In a few weeks time, Ray notified Jeremy that the project was ready to be marketed. Jeremy began corresponding with hundreds of cruise ship lines, but only one responded favorably. Most of the others either didn't respond at all or wrote to him saying how such a device seemed preposterous or they even used stronger language. The one respondent that seemed interested was the Century Cruise Lines. One of its ships had a kitchen fire a few months ago and all the passengers had to assemble in the area near where the life jackets were, just in case the ship needed to be evacuated. Fortunately, the fire was extinguished by an alert crew, but the episode put a scare in the passengers.

After word got around about this particular ship's fire, the cruise line noticed that customers were specifying they did not wish to go on it. Since this was a new ship and the fire did little damage, the captain convinced the Century Lines to order the Life Saver. His ship would be the only one to have this new feature and this could be a way to attract prospective passengers. Century Lines ordered three thousand Life Savers for this particular ship and it proved to be a wise move.

When people saw the ad that Century put out describing the advantages of the Life Saver, the ship began receiving a heavy volume of bookings, so much so, that captains of other ships in the Century Line wanted them. When other cruise lines heard about the Life Saver, they started to place orders, also.

Since the Life Saver was so small, there was no way cruise lines could have passengers turn them back in, so the Life Saver became a virtual souvenir, which could be used in the future by anyone who was into boating of any kind.

Eventually, the Navy and the Coast Guard began ordering the Life Saver. Swim Works, now owned by Robox, had to go to a third shift just to keep up with the unexpected heavy demand. The employees were thrilled with all this work since they had been expecting layoffs before Robox stepped in. Both companies were in a win-win situation.

As summer got into full swing, yacht clubs all over the country were buying the Life Saver for their members. People who like to do their Christmas shopping early were also buying them.

The *Yachtsman*, a favorite magazine of yacht owners, not only had a Life Saver ad in it every month, but one issue had a real life story of a yacht that began sinking one night when all the passengers were asleep. The owner's son, who was only seven years old, was awakened by water touching his face and, realizing what was happening, inflated his Life Saver. He immediately shouted to the others onboard to wake up and inflate their Life Savers, which were attached to whatever type of clothing they had on. As the yacht was sinking, everyone jumped overboard and began screaming for help. Since they were just off shore and other boats were nearby, they were all rescued in a matter of minutes. The Life Saver certainly prevented a tragedy that night.

Accompanying the story was a picture of the yacht owner and his family with Ray and Jeremy being identified as representatives of the Robox Company, the producer of the Life Saver.

With sales of the Life Saver being so successful, Ray thought he would attempt to come up with another life saving product that had to do with water safety. He actually had thought of this long before Robox purchased Swim Works, but now the time seemed even more appropriate.

Jeremy happened to come by this one day when Ray was working in the design room and asked him, "are you working on something new?"

"I am. You will never guess what it is."

"I bet it's a boat that won't sink," said Jeremy jokingly.

"You're close. It's a boot that won't sink. You will actually be able to walk on water, if I can pull it off the way I think I can."

"How can you do something that has never been done since the time of Jesus?"

"Jesus didn't need what I am trying to develop. He was able to walk on water by his own powers."

"Tell me what you have in mind for this boot?"

"My theory is for the boot to be constructed in such a way that the water comes in through little portholes along the lower sides of the boot and is quickly extracted out the upper sides of the boot, so that there is a continuous flow of water that creates buoyancy in the boot."

"That makes sense to me, but can you really make it work?"

"I'll know in a few days when I bring it over to R&D for testing."

"Let me play the devil's advocate here. Suppose you have people walking on water all over the place, won't there be a possibility they might get hit by a passing boat?"

"If these are used at all by boaters, it would mainly be in an emergency situation, such as, when a boat needs to be evacuated. In that case, passengers would be expecting to have another boat nearby to rescue them, or at least give them more time to wait for help to arrive."

"In what other situations would they be used?"

"Well, lifeguards could use them if a swimmer were drowning."

"Wouldn't the boot just sink due to the weight of the person wearing it?"

"The boot will have a large flat surface attached to it, similar to the size of a snowshoe. This will add to the boot's buoyancy. For example, fishermen, who wade in the water up to their hips, would be able to go out further than they can now. The boot will also be equipped with levelers in case of rough seas and will have spikes attached when used on icy surfaces."

"This could be difficult to market. There would be a lot of skeptics as people hear about this product."

"We have dealt with skeptics before, haven't we? But we always seem to find someone willing to try our new products, don't we?"

"I guess you're right. I'll begin working on the marketing end of it right away. It's going to be a real challenge."

Jeremy kept in constant touch with Ray and waited until the testing was completed before he contacted the ad department. When the ad finally came out it pictured a family walking on water with the special boots prominently displayed. The name given to this new product was the Water Walker. Anyone wanting it would need to call the Robox Company for more information.

The first call came from a company in Georgia that conducted a ferry service across a narrow river that separated two small towns. Due to expensive upkeep and rising fuel costs, the company was on the verge of bankruptcy. The owners thought that, from what they read in the ad, the Water Walker might be the answer to their financial problems, so they called Robox and ordered one hundred boots.

Their new operation consisted of renting out the Water Walker for $5.00 per river crossing, so customers could walk across instead of being ferried. For added safety, the company installed a railing that stretched across the river to give people a chance to hold on to something in case they felt uneasy or distrustful of the special boots. On each side of the river was a small building which housed fifty boots of various sizes and had an attendant present to help the customers. Many people rented the boots just to discover the experience of walking on water and most found it to be a fun thing to do. The unusual novelty brought curiosity seekers along the river's edge to watch the people walking on the water. The company thrived on this new venture and, thanks to the Water Walker, saved itself from financial ruin.

There was another situation in New Hampshire one late fall day. Emergency personnel had been called to a lake where a small dog had fallen through a thin layer of ice. The rescue effort was failing because of a delay in a police boat not being dispatched to the scene soon enough. All of a sudden a man stopped his car to find out what all the commotion was on the lake. It happened to be someone who had just bought a pair of Water Walkers very recently and hadn't had a chance to even use them. He opened the trunk of his car, put on the boots and walked right along the ice to where the dog was. He then picked up the frozen wet and frightened little animal and brought him to shore. Everyone was amazed at this unorthodox rescue method, especially the police and firemen at the scene.

As the dog was being wrapped in a blanket, one of the rescue workers asked the man, "where did you ever get those funny looking boots? They really saved the day for this poor little fellow. I noticed you were able to stay up even as the ice broke beneath you. Where can we get those boots? We could certainly use them with all the lakes we have in these parts."

"All you have to do is call the Robox Company," replied the man, "their toll free number is right on my boots. They'll tell you where you can buy them. I bought mine directly through the company."

Another bystander who witnessed this whole scenario, had his video camera taking in all the action. He happened to be a newsman for the local television station, so he aired the whole story on the evening news. It was even shown on the national evening news, since the station was an affiliate of a national network.

The next day, Robox was swamped with calls seeking information on where these boots could be purchased. Jeremy was even handling calls due to the great volume. When he finally had the opportunity, he talked to Ray and said, "I think it's time to have our retail stores fully stocked with the Water Walkers. It seems, after last night's national television exposure, the demand for them is going to be tremendous. Those workers at Swim Works are going to need a third shift for a long time to come."

Over the next decade, Ray came up with many other new creations for the Robox Company and Jeremy was right there handling the marketing of them. Before they left the company for retirement, Robox honored them both with a much deserved banquet. They were each presented with a plaque with an inscription praising their many contributions to the company.

Author Biography

Raymond Fell has authored four books to date. *An Athlete's Fantasy* is his latest sports fiction story. Because religion, family and sports are so very close to his heart, he has written *Go To Heaven*, *Judgment Day* and *A Football Player's Dream*. A competitive road racer for the past 25 years, Raymond has participated in over 250 races as well as in the National Senior Games. He is looking forward to the 2009 nationals which will be held in San Francisco and to the 2011 games in Houston. Raymond plans to run in the 5K and 10K races as an octogenarian.

Printed in the United States
204464BV00001B/466-489/P

9 781434 394835